Sergeant Casey Wheeler
69th Regiment
A.E.F.
A.P.O. 702

The Honorable Uncle Sam
The Government
Washington, District of Columbia

CASEY
OVER THERE

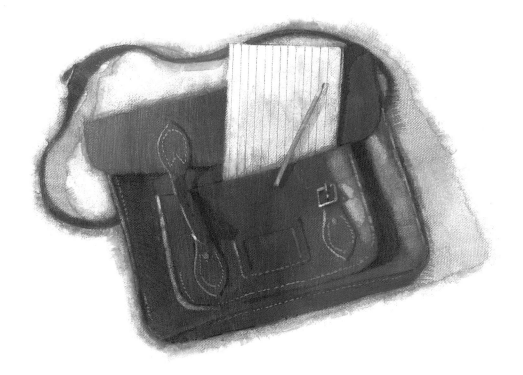

WRITTEN BY

Staton Rabin

ILLUSTRATED BY

Greg Shed

Harcourt Brace & Company

San Diego   New York   London

Library of Congress Cataloging-in-Publication Data
Rabin, Staton.
Casey over there/by Staton Rabin; illustrated by Greg Shed.—1st ed.
p.   cm.
Summary: After his older brother Casey goes off to fight in
World War I, Aubrey and his family are so worried that Aubrey writes a
letter to Uncle Sam asking him to send Casey home.
ISBN 0–15–253186–6
[1. World War, 1914–1918—Fiction. 2. Brothers—Fiction.]
I. Shed, Greg, ill. II. Title.
PZ7.R1084Cas   1994
[E]—dc20   92-30322

First edition
A B C D E

Printed in Singapore

The paintings in this book were done in designer gouache on canvas.
The display type was set in Bodoni Poster Highlight by Photo-lettering, Inc., New York, New York.
The text type was set in Fournier by Thompson Type, San Diego, California.
Aubrey's letters were hand-lettered by Alex Peters.
Casey's letter was hand-lettered by Judythe Sieck.
Color separations were made by Bright Arts, Ltd., Singapore.
Printed and bound by Tien Wah Press, Singapore
Production supervision by Warren Wallerstein and David Hough
Designed by Trina Stahl

WHEN AUBREY was seven, his brother Casey joined the army.

Aubrey thought Uncle Sam was a little like Santa Claus, only skinnier and taller and not so jolly. He made people think of America, the way Santa reminds people of Christmas. If Uncle Sam wanted you, you went.

Aubrey was too young to go. But Casey wasn't, so he sailed to France to fight in the Great War.

Letters and packages took a long time to cross the Atlantic Ocean. There Aubrey was in Brooklyn, writing another letter to Casey asking, "Did you get it yet?"

And there Casey was in Broussey, waiting for the package
Aubrey had sent two months ago.

There was Casey, dipping his helmet into a muddy trench
for water to shave with.

And there was Aubrey, playing kick the can on West 9th Street, wondering if Casey ever got the shaving soap.

Dear Runt,
     Don't need soap after all. Red Cross had some. Please send chewing gum instead (Black Jack or nothing).

Love,
Your brother
(Sergeant Casey Wheeler)
69th New York

Soldier Mail

Dear Sergeant Casey
(I like the sound of that),
     Too late.

Love,
Aubrey

Aubrey's family went to Coney Island one Sunday. They thought being busy might help them stop worrying about Casey for a few hours. Mrs. Wheeler worried anyway, and Aubrey got sick on the Ferris wheel.

Aubrey and his father rolled up their pants legs and waded
into the ocean. A man in a striped bathing suit walked up and
down the beach like he wanted to show off his muscles. And a
fox terrier ate Aubrey's saltwater taffy.

"Is Casey over there on the other side?" Aubrey asked
his father.

"That's France. Yes, indeed."

"I'm waving to him, Dad."

The months dripped by. Casey got trench foot from sitting in the mud.

Aubrey sprained his ankle playing king of the hill. Mrs. Wheeler
gave up bridge and went to church more often.

The mailbox was empty again. Three months since the last letter from Casey. Aubrey was very worried. So he wrote another letter.

Dear Uncle Sam,
    My brother is in the Fighting 69th (Sergeant Casey Wheeler is his name). Over there, like the song says. Are you done with him yet?
        Yours very truly,
        Aubrey Wheeler

"What's his address?" Aubrey asked.

Mr. Wheeler looked up from the *New York Times* and slid his eyeglasses to the tip of his nose.

"I don't know, Aubrey." He reached over and scratched Aubrey's favorite itchy shoulder blade. "I don't know if . . . Uncle Sam answers his mail. He's pretty busy, I imagine."

"Isn't Santa Claus busy?"

Aubrey's father shrugged. "In December, anyway."

"And doesn't he answer my letters every Christmas?"

"Um . . . well, he certainly seems to, doesn't he?" Mr. Wheeler said.

Aubrey followed Mr. Zadikow all the way to the post office to make sure the letter didn't fall out of his mailbag. On the envelope he'd written:

The Honorable Uncle Sam
The Government
Washington, District of Columbia

Soon the leaves on the Wheelers' trees turned red and yellow. One day there was a knock on the front door, and Mrs. Wheeler nearly fainted.

"Sorry I gave you a start, Mrs. Wheeler," said Mr. Zadikow, wiping his feet on the straw mat. "It's not a telegram—don't worry." A telegram could mean Casey had been killed in the war.

"It's for you, kid," Mr. Zadikow said to Aubrey, handing
him the envelope. "From Washington."

Aubrey tore the envelope open so fast he ripped the letter
in two. He held the pieces together to read it.

November 24, 1917

Dear Aubrey,

I hope you won't be disappointed to receive a reply from me rather than from the honorable old gentleman. Uncle Sam is much occupied with the war effort at present, and my secretary surmised that I might be the next best thing to the genuine article.

I want you to know how proud I am to have fine young men like your brother, Sergeant Casey Wheeler, serving our country. I'm sure you are proud of him, too. And I can only begin to imagine how much he is missed. As for Sergeant Wheeler, he is fortunate indeed to have a brother who is so determined to look out for his welfare.

I wish I could send him home to you tomorrow. Alas, Uncle Sam is not through with him yet. When he is, I imagine I should be one of the first to know.

Until then, I wish you and yours peace of mind. And, for all of us, a world at peace that is safe for democracy once more.

Sincerely yours,

Woodrow Wilson

Aubrey chewed up a stick of Black Jack and used it to fasten the two halves of President Wilson's letter back together. The letter took a place of honor on Aubrey's bedroom wall, next to his photo of Mary Pickford, his favorite movie star. He read the letter every night before he went to sleep.

But he still missed Casey.

There was Aubrey, flattening pennies under the wheels of the trolley in Brooklyn.

And there was Casey, crawling on his belly, leading a patrol into no-man's-land.

Nearly a year went by. And then, at the eleventh hour of the eleventh day of the eleventh month of 1918 . . .

Aubrey and his parents met Casey down by the piers.
He was thin, and he had a limp.

"Casey?"

"Yeah, runt."

"When you were in France, did you see me wave to you that time from Coney Island?"

"Sure," Casey said. "Why'd you think I waved back?"

My father grew up in Brooklyn shortly after Aubrey did. He remembers walking the beach at Coney Island and flattening pennies under the wheels of passing trolleys. But then, like Casey, he was sent far from home to fight in a big and terrible war. Neither Aubrey nor Casey is a real person; my father's life inspired me to create them.

President Wilson asked Congress to declare war on Germany in April 1917. Though the infantry regiment called the Fighting 69th was among the first American troops sent "over there," it arrived in France in the fall and fought no battles until 1918. I compressed that time frame for the sake of my story.

At least since the days of Lincoln—when 11-year-old Grace Bedell urged the Republican candidate to grow a beard (and Old Abe took her advice)—children have been writing to their president. Did Woodrow Wilson ever receive a letter like the one Aubrey wrote to "Uncle Sam"? I can't prove that he did. But this much is certain: President Wilson liked and respected children.

Just before the United States declared war on Germany, Wilson was out walking with a lifelong friend, Edith Gittings Reid. They were stopped by a young newspaper boy. "There ain't going to be no war," pleaded the deeply worried child. "Mr. President, tell Mr. Kaiser he got to stop. War done bust."

Mrs. Reid smiled and asked the astonished president, "Is that the voice of the people?"

"Upon my word," Wilson replied, "I believe it is. If the politicians and potentates, all of us, handed the whole business over to that little chap we would have peace in twenty-four hours."

I have no doubt that if Aubrey's letter had found its way onto Woodrow Wilson's desk, the president would have answered it.

—STATON RABIN

The Honorable Uncle Sam
The Govern
Washington, District

69th Regi
A.E.F.
A.P.O. 702

Sergeant Case
69th Regiment
A.E.F.
A.P.O. 702

Soldier Mail

Aubrey
West 9
rooklyn,

Sergeant Casey Wheeler
69th Regiment
A.E.F.
A.P.O. 702